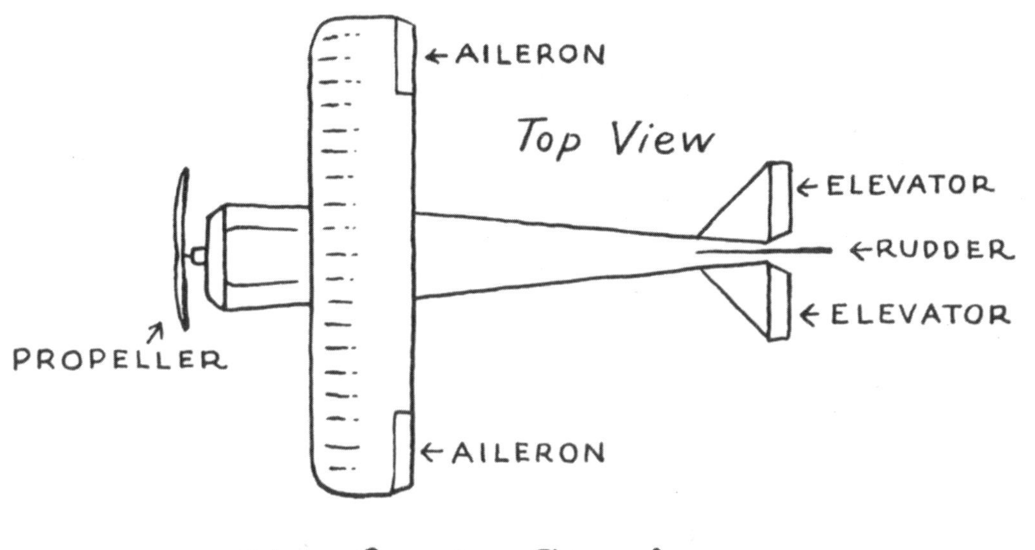

The Little Airplane

 Published in the United States by Random House Children's Books, a division of Random House, Inc., New York, and simultaneously in Canada by Random House of Canada Limited, Toronto.
Originally published by Henry Z. Walck, Inc., in 1938.

www.randomhouse.com/kids

Library of Congress Cataloging-in-Publication Data
Lenski, Lois, 1893–1974
The little airplane / by Lois Lenski.
p. cm.
Summary: Pilot Small flies his airplane over the countryside, does a loop-the-loop, makes an emergency landing, and finally returns safely to the hangar.
[1. Air pilots—Fiction.] I. Title.
PZ7.L54 Ld 2003
[E]—dc21
2001041763
ISBN 0-375-81079-X (trade) — ISBN 0-375-91079-4 (lib. bdg.)

Printed in the United States of America 10 9 8 7 6 5 4 3 2 1
First Random House Edition

The LITTLE AIRPLANE

LOIS LENSKI

Random House New York

Pilot Small has a little airplane. He keeps it in the hangar at the airport.

TINYTOWN
AIRPORT

It is a fine, sunny day. Pilot Small and the mechanic roll the airplane out of the hangar. Pilot Small decides to go up. They look the motor over carefully. They fill the tanks with gas.

GAS

All is ready for the takeoff. Pilot Small climbs into the cockpit and sits down. He fastens his safety belt. He looks round on all sides to make sure the field is clear.

Pilot Small pumps the throttle a few times to prime the engine. The mechanic winds the propeller until the gas gets into the motor. Then he calls, "Contact!" Pilot Small turns on the switch and answers, "Contact!" The mechanic pulls the propeller through and it starts whizzing. The engine starts with a loud roar.

Pilot Small races the engine a few times. It roars loudly. He releases the brake. He looks at the wind indicator to see which way the wind is blowing. He taxis to the end of the field, in order to bring the plane round into the wind. He keeps the stick back to raise the elevators. The wind pressure on them keeps the plane down.

TINYTOW
AIRPORT

Now he is ready to take off. The motor is warmed up. He allows the stick to go forward gradually, until the tail-skid lifts. When flying speed is reached, he pulls back gently on the stick. This raises the elevators and lifts the plane off the ground. The plane climbs steeply into the wind.

The little airplane rises in the air. Pilot Small looks down and watches the ground slip away beneath him. He keeps one hand on the gas.

TOWN
AIRPORT

Up and up the little airplane goes until it reaches a height of 2,000 feet. Pilot Small pushes the stick halfway forward, into neutral, to level off. The plane flies along smoothly.

Pilot Small decides to make a right turn. He pushes the stick to the right. This lowers the aileron on the left wing and raises the aileron on the right wing. At the same time, he presses on the rudder bar with his right foot, turning the rudder to the right. The plane banks as it turns to the right. Then he straightens the rudder and puts the stick back to neutral, to come out of the turn. He continues on a straight course.

NC17140

The little airplane flies over a large lake. It hits the air pocket and drops thirty feet. The jolt gives Pilot Small an empty feeling in his stomach, but he does not mind. He flies low over the lake. He peeps out and sees his little Sailboat rocking at anchor beneath him. He speeds up his motor and the little airplane climbs again.

The little airplane flies over a town. Pilot Small sees the people walking about like little ants on the streets below.

The little airplane climbs higher and higher. It climbs up through open holes in the clouds toward the blue sky above. It flies above the clouds. Pilot Small likes this the best of all! He sees the clouds like layers and layers of cotton beneath him. It is a very beautiful sight!

The little airplane glides down through the clouds. It sinks gently through the foggy, dry mist. Now it is below the clouds. Pilot Small sees the ground appear again beneath him.

Pilot Small decides to do a loop. He pushes the throttle wide open to gain speed. He puts the stick forward to put the nose down. He pulls back on the stick gradually. The little airplane dives first, then climbs up sharply, turns over, and comes back to its first position. Pilot Small is pushed down into his seat. He gasps for breath, then gives a chuckle. He feels very proud of himself. He does another loop just for fun!

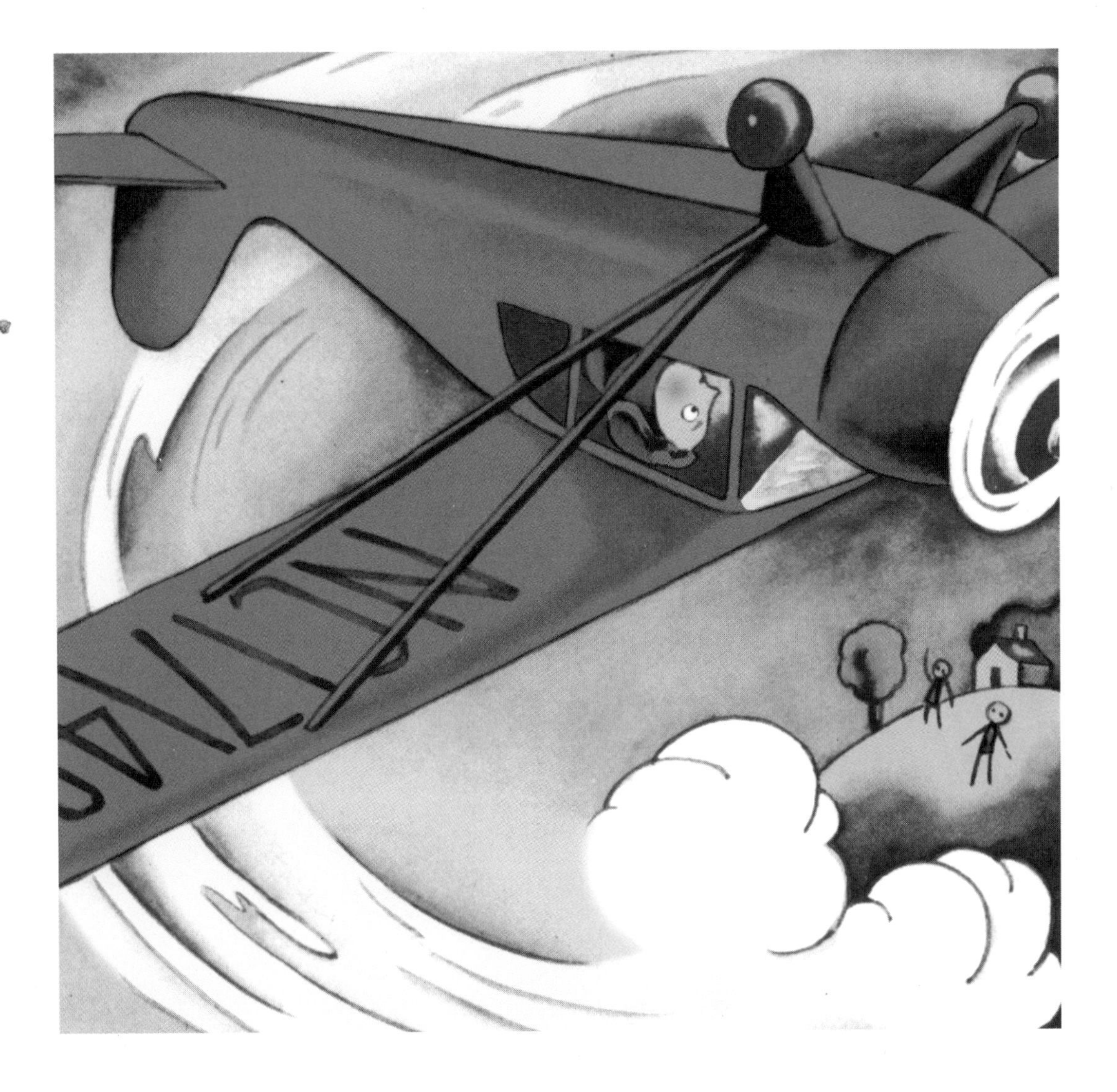

Just then the engine begins
to sputter. *Chuck-a, chuck-a,
chuck-a-a*— It stops dead. The
gas line is clogged. The little
airplane glides and begins
to sink slowly. Pilot Small looks
worried.

Pilot Small looks for a safe landing place. He sees an open field at the edge of a dense forest. Perhaps it is a swamp. Perhaps it is full of rocks and stones. He hopes not, for he will have to make a forced landing.

The little airplane glides to the ground. It lands safely in a grassy field. Pilot Small climbs out of the cockpit. He takes tools from his toolbox. He fixes the gas line and his motor begins to hum once more. What a relief! Pilot Small smiles broadly. He takes off again. Away goes the little airplane!

It is growing late. Pilot Small banks again to return. He flies back to the airport. He flies low over his home. He sees his fields, his house, and his garage. Circling above the airport, he sees his little Auto waiting for him beside the hangar.

The flight is over. Pilot Small decides to land. He circles to the right of the field. He looks at the wind indicator to see which way the wind is blowing. He decides on a point on the field that he wishes to hit and keeps his eye on it. He throttles his motor down to lose speed. He glides down against the wind.

TOWN
AIRPORT.

As he comes close to the ground, he pulls the stick back to level off. The little airplane drops to the ground. It makes a perfect three-point landing. The two wheels and the tail-skid hit the ground at the same moment.

Pilot Small sets one brake and turns round. He taxis, *bumpety-bump*, to the hangar. He shuts off the motor. The propeller stops. He opens the door of the cockpit and steps out.

Pilot Small and the mechanic roll
the little airplane into the hangar.
Pilot Small jumps into his little
Auto and drives off!

AIRPORT

And that's all

about Pilot Small!

AIRPORT
AIRPORT